# Bedtime Stories for Lovers

### Joan Elizabeth Lloyd

**WARNER BOOKS**

A Time Warner Company

Warner Books, Inc., 1271 Avenue of the Americas, New York, NY 10020

**W** A Time Warner Company

Printed in the United States of America

ISBN 0-446-67139-8

Book design, composition and text illustrations by Giorgetta Bell McRee
Cover design by Cathy Saksa
Cover photograph by Cathy Saksa

*This book is dedicated to my personal storyteller with all my love.*

*Once Ed begins to whisper an erotic tale like the ones in this book into my ear, sleep becomes the furthest thing from my mind.*

*How wonderful.*

# Contents

Dear Reader,

Some of my most wonderful childhood memories begin with my parents' soft voices saying, "Once upon a time. . . ." Listening to their words, I traveled through the woods with Goldilocks, to work in the mines with the Seven Dwarfs, and into the witch's hut with Hansel and Gretel.

As I grew older, my bedtime imaginings evolved. They included horseback riding with Bobby Bensen and the B-Bar-B Riders, then flying with Sky King. After that came driving around the country on Route 66 and, eventually, being comforted by Dr. Kildare or Ben Casey. And, in the wonderful world of my fantasies, I could be anyone, do anything, and look any way I chose. I could be the smartest girl in the world or the best trick horseback rider. I could fly. I could have long, straight jet black hair and light blue eyes. I could even be shapely enough to fill out a bra.

Eventually, of course, my fantasies turned to lovemaking. In my imagination, I could be loved by the most talented suitor in an endless variety of ways. He would "just know" exactly what I wanted and when I wanted it. Anything was possible. My fantasies turned me on. When I finally mustered the courage to share them with my

partner, they enhanced our lovemaking, and ulti-
mately, most of them came true.

Can your fantasies come true? Emphatically, I
say yes. But you may have to help your partner to
understand what you'd enjoy. He won't "just
know." You can use this book to give your partner
the nudge that will allow the two of you to share
your most exotic desires.

This book contains many of my favorite fantasies, in fairy-tale form. And, I'm sure that many
of these fantasies are yours, too. Have you ever
dreamed of making love in the daytime on a blanket under a deserted bridge? Or making love surrounded by the smell and feel of rich, soft leather?
Have you dreamed of owning a pair of boots that
will give you the courage to take control of your
relationship? Or of giving those boots to your
partner and giving up control? If you have, you're
in good company.

There are several different ways you can turn
your secret dreams into delicious reality. First,
you can read these stories and let these ideas, sit-
uations, and images inspire you. Let these scenar-
ios turn you on. Now climb into bed with your
partner and enjoy. Go a little wild. Do things
you've never done before.

A second way to enjoy these stories is to read

one out loud at bedtime. Force yourself to say those naughty words or ask your partner to read a story to you. It's wonderfully embarrassing and exciting. Then see what happens next.

Third, you can use these stories to suggest a new activity to your partner. Tell your partner something wonderful by slipping a bookmark into a particular story. Help your partner to understand that this is a situation you'd like to act out, together. It's a small risk that can lead to a big reward.

However you use this book, read, relax, and enjoy. And remember that everyone has fantasies. Have the courage to share yours with a loving partner. You might just find yourself embarking on adventures even more tantalizing than anything you've ever imagined.

# Bedtime Stories for Lovers

# Mirror, Mirror

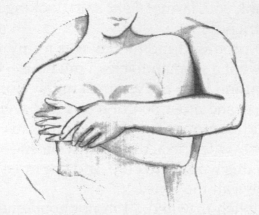

Once upon a time, there was a handsome farmer named Dalton who had always prayed for a beautiful woman who would cook for him, raise his children, and, of course, have such a fantastic body that they would make love all the time. One day, on his way to his fields, he met a young, good witch who had her foot caught under a large rock. "Help me," the witch cried. "Please, young man, if you free me, you'll find that I'm the answer to all your prayers."

"You're very skinny and not very beautiful," the farmer said, "so you couldn't be the answer to my prayers. However, I'll get you out of there, anyway." Using all his strength, he freed the witch's foot.

"Thank you, farmer," she said, looking over his warm, friendly face.

"You promised me the answer to my prayers. Well, I want a woman to clean my house, bear my children, and keep me warm at night. Unlike you, of course, she must be gorgeous and well-built." He held his cupped hands in front of his chest to show the witch exactly how well endowed he wanted this woman to be. "And she must want to make love all the time."

The witch frowned. "I'm not good enough for you?"

"Not a chance," Dalton said, holding his hands in front of his chest. "Big. Really big."

"If that's truly what you want," the witch said, hooking her index fingers together and blinking her eyes, "then this evening you will find an enchanted mirror hanging in your bedroom. From it will emerge the girl of your dreams."

That evening, Dalton couldn't wait to get home. He ran up the stairs and, on his bedroom wall, he found a full-length mirror. "Where's my dream woman?" he asked out loud. Suddenly, the mirror became cloudy and from its depths a beautiful and extremely well-endowed naked woman materialized. "I've been waiting for you all afternoon," she murmured, wrapping her arms around Dalton's waist.

"Wow." He sighed. As he reached for her, he silently thanked the witch for rewarding him so generously.

The woman's hands were everywhere. She unbuttoned his shirt and stroked his hairy chest, kissing and licking his flat nipples. "Oh, love," she groaned as she pushed him onto the bed, "you're so sexy." She straddled his chest, took his hand, and placed it on one large breast, holding it tightly against her so Dalton could fill his hand with her flesh. "Your hands feel so good." While she rubbed her wet cunt against his chest, she lifted his other hand and filled it with her other large breast. "Yes. So good."

Dalton closed his eyes and let the beautiful girl use his hands to stroke her body. When she placed his hand palm up on his flat stomach and sat on it, he thought his cock would burst from his pants. His fingers tangled in her sopping fur and two fingers slipped inside her cunt.

"Oh, baby," he groaned. "Let me fuck you."

"Of course." She opened his pants' buttons and impaled herself on his stiff erection. Up and down, up and down—she rode him until he could hold back no longer. He arched his back and thick come filled her pussy. Exhausted, he collapsed.

As if this wasn't enough, she got up and announced, "Now I'll cook you a good meal." Patting his now-flaccid cock, she continued, "Then you'll be ready to do this again."

The meal was perfect, and when they were done eating, they made love again.

For several weeks, Dalton spent very little time in his fields. Every minute was spent either eating or making love. Finally, he had had enough. "Oh, witch," he cried, lying exhausted on the bed while his lover was in the kitchen. "Witch, please answer me." From the depths of the cloudy mirror, the witch stepped into the small room. "Oh, witch," he moaned, "this is awful. She won't let me alone. She wants me to fondle her tits all the time, sometimes even when she's cooking. I've gained five pounds and I'm so tired that I haven't the strength to get anything done. Help me." He knelt on the floor at the witch's feet and hugged her knees. "Please."

"Well," the witch said, "she is what you said you wanted."

Dalton hung his head. "I know." He sighed. "But she never lets me give her pleasure. She never shares in bed. It's not really fun anymore." He looked over the witch's small but well-formed body. "And she doesn't talk, or play cards, or read. She just cooks, holds my hands on her big breasts, and fucks."

"She's not what you wanted?"

Dalton sat on the side of the bed. "She's what I thought I wanted. I guess I was wrong."

The witch smiled. "I play gin rummy, and I like to read. I'm a decent cook, and together we can learn how good it can be in bed." She winked at him. "And I think you're very special and very handsome."

Dalton took the witch's hand. "I like you, too." Suddenly, he heard footsteps on the stairs. "Oh no, here she comes."

"Dalton, darling," the young woman's voice called as she entered the room with a tray of hors d'oeuvres. "I've got something to tide you over until dinner." She started to set the tray on the table and opened her shirt to reveal her large tits.

The witch looked at Dalton, and when he nodded, she hooked her index fingers together and blinked her eyes. The woman disappeared. Then the witch blinked again and a deck of cards appeared in her hand. "How about we share some of those lovely treats while I beat you at gin?"

"Wonderful," Dalton said, knowing that he had found a woman with many wonderful tricks up her sleeve.

# Magic Boots

"My wife is such a shy little thing," King Carl said to his grand wizard. "She lets me love her but seems to get no pleasure from it. I do everything and she submits. She acts more like a dutiful subject than my consort."

The wizard thought about Queen Myra and had to agree with the king. She was lovely, but she lacked spirit. "And you would like . . ."

"I'd like her to be active in the bedroom, suggest things, make things happen. You know . . ."

"I think I do," the wizard said. He rummaged around in an old trunk and pulled out a pair of high-heeled lace-up boots. He handed them to the king and said, "Sire, give these to your wife for her birthday next week. Do it when the two of you are alone, after everyone else has gone to bed."

"What will they do?" King Carl asked.

"You'll see," was all the wizard would say.

At the dinner for his wife's birthday, King Carl gave her a jeweled tiara and an aquamarine pendant that was the exact color of her eyes. During a long dinner, she received dozens of other gifts, one more glorious than the next. She accepted each gift with grace and quiet dignity.

Finally, after all the guests were gone, the couple sat in the dining hall. The king brought out his special gift. "One last gift," he said as he handed the box to her.

Queen Myra opened the box and pulled out the old scuffed boots. "I don't understand," she said softly.

"Neither do I, but put them on. Please."

With a shrug, the queen pulled the high boots on and smoothed the supple leather up her calves. She took a deep breath and crossed her legs. "Lace them up for me," she said, her words almost an order.

Startled, the king knelt at her feet and threaded the laces through the dozens of eyelets. As he went to tie the first one, Myra snapped, "Tighter."

Bemused, he tightened the laces, tied the top, and then laced and tied the other boot. Now what? he wondered. He didn't have long to wait. "Get undressed," Myra commanded.

"What?"

"You heard me," she said, picking up a linen napkin, twirling it into a rope, and snapping it at him. "Now!"

As quickly as he could, the king removed his clothes, until he stood before his wife totally naked. She snapped the napkin against the king's erect cock, which stuck out from his groin. "That's going to have to wait," she said, lifting her skirts. She picked up a knife from the table, cut through the sides of her panties, and pulled the silk from between her thighs. "Pleasure me," she said to her flabbergasted husband.

"Oh yes, my dear." He knelt between her knees and slid his hands up the soft white skin inside her thighs. His thumbs reached her cunt and gently parted her flesh.

As she slid forward to give him better access

to her slippery flesh, she looped the napkin around the back of his neck and pulled him toward her. "Do it," she growled.

Eagerly, he buried his face in her musky cunt and licked at her swollen clitoris. "Gently," she said. "Lick along the slit, then flick your tongue over my clit." As he found her rhythm, she settled back into her chair. "Yes," she purred, "that's good. Faster now."

He complied, feeling her excitement rise. Her juices flowed from her body, bathing his tongue in her salty fluid. She used the cloth to hold his head against her until, with a scream, she came. Panting, she relaxed her hold on him.

"Oh, darling," she said, "I've never felt like that before—so powerful, so able to take what I wanted."

"I know. The wizard promised that those boots would have an invigorating effect on our sex life, but I never expected . . ."

"The wizard?"

"I told him about our love life and how I wanted you to take a more active role. He gave me the enchanted boots to give to you."

Queen Myra leaned forward and snapped the napkin across the king's naked buttocks. "You talked about our sex life. You really must be punished for that."

The king laughed and bowed down before her. "Yes," he said. "Your wishes are my commands."

# The Cobbler

One night, a poor cobbler who made shoes for the residents of a small village received a message from a mysterious visitor who bade him make a pair of shoes each month and leave it on his workbench on the night of the full moon. "Good fortune and happiness will be yours," the message said. For three months, he did as he was asked, and he now had more customers than he could handle and money enough for all the things he had ever wanted.

Whom shall I thank? he wondered. So one full-moon night, he hid in his cobbler shop and watched. At precisely midnight, a beautiful girl dressed in a green gown magically appeared and quickly slipped the new shoes onto her feet. For almost an hour, she danced around the shop to music that only she could hear. Then, as mysteriously as she had appeared, she vanished.

For the next month, the cobbler was obsessed with her beautiful face, her full breasts and long legs. So the next full-moon night, he hid, and when the girl appeared, he slowly moved from his hiding place behind a pile of hides. "You like my shoes?" he asked softly.

At first, the girl appeared frightened, but as the cobbler approached, his warm smile calmed and then excited her. "Yes, very much," she said finally. "The soft leather caresses my feet and I dance to feel their magic. Then I return to my people and give the shoes to their new owner."

"You like the feel of leather?" the cobbler asked.

"I love the look and the feel and the smell," she said. "And I love the way your strong hands can shape and smooth it into shoes and boots. I watch you often from my secret place."

"There are other ways to enjoy leather," the cobbler said, already hungry for the girl's body. "I would love to show you."

The girl looked at the bulge beneath the cobbler's apron and smiled. Slowly, he approached her, and as he held her, he became aware that she was naked under her gown. Smiling, the cobbler drew her gown over the girl's head, picked her up, and sat her down, naked, on the pile of hides. "Feel the leather on your naked ass," he whispered. "Smell the fragrance of the new skins."

As the girl lay back, the smooth leather caressed her body from calves to head. As the cobbler watched, she turned over and moved her body sinuously across the hides, rubbing her breasts and belly on the leather. When she turned back over, her nipples were swollen and her arms reached out for him. "Love me here," she said. When the cobbler had pulled off his clothes, the girl could clearly see that his hard cock was ready to plunge into her. "Fill me with your hard cock while I fill my senses with this wonderful leather."

Quickly, the cobbler lay beside her body and slid his hands over her blazing flesh. As his fingers slid between her spread legs, he felt her wetness and knew she was ready for him. He levered himself up on his elbows and knees and positioned his erection at the dripping entrance to her hungry body.

Unable to wait, the girl wrapped her legs around the cobbler's waist and pulled him into her. As he loved her, he took the corner of the topmost hide and stretched it across her face, beneath her nose, so she was enveloped by the smell of the newly tanned skin.

Harder and harder, he plunged into the girl's tight channel until neither could hold back any longer. They moaned as they came almost simultaneously.

Later, when their breathing had calmed, the girl said, "I'll come here every full-moon night. Will you be waiting for me?"

"Oh yes," the cobbler said. "And I'll make some special leather clothing for you to wear while we make love."

Now, each full-moon night the villagers hear squeals and giggles and the sounds of lovemaking coming from the cobbler's shop. And occasionally, the cobbler can be seen dancing to music only he can hear.

# The Princess Tests

"Well, son," the king said, "Princess Amanda has passed all the princess tests so far—looks, dress, manners, poise."

"I know," Prince Mark said, "she's perfect for me. I've spent a lot of time with Amanda, and, Father, I know that I want to marry her."

"There's one test left," Queen Bertrice said.

"There is?" the prince said. "I've not heard of any more tests."

"The test of vulnerability," the queen continued. "I will go into her room this afternoon and place a pebble under her mattress. She must be so delicate that it bruises her skin."

"That's ridiculous," Mark said. "No one could pass that test."

"That's the way it is," the queen said. "And if she doesn't pass, we'll have to send her packing and try another candidate." She looked at her husband, the king. "Do you agree, my lord?"

"I certainly do," the king said to his son. "She must pass all the princess tests in order to be allowed to marry you."

Prince Mark sighed. One last test and Amanda will be mine. I'll make sure she passes.

"And no cheating," Queen Bertrice said. "I want your promise that you won't tell her anything. Not one word. Promise me."

"Not one word," Prince Mark said, his mind already wrestling with the problem. "I won't tell her a thing. You have my promise."

Late that evening, Prince Mark made his way through the halls of the palace and tiptoed quietly into the princess's room. Amanda lay curled on her side, sound asleep, her long dark hair spread on the snowy pillow, her shape barely visible in the low light from the fireplace. Mark slipped out of his clothes and slid between the fine silk sheets.

nt to look at you, too. And we'll be married
, anyway."

he prince placed Amanda's smooth naked
y on the bricks of the hearth, appreciating the
the firelight made her skin glow as if lit from
in. "Ouch," she squealed. "The bricks are a
ncomfortable." When Mark placed his mouth
he tiny bud between her thighs and sucked
ly, she forgot any discomfort. He licked the
th of her moist slit, then sucked her clit into
mouth again. "Darling," she moaned, "take
ow. I'm so hungry for you."

Yes, my love," he said, lifting her legs over his
lders and ramming his cock into her waiting
nel. Over and over, he pounded while she
d her hips to meet his thrusts. At the moment
eir simultaneous climax, he dropped her legs
covered her mouth with his, muffling their
of ecstasy.

Vhen their breathing returned to normal,
ce Mark took a soft cloth and cleaned
anda's body and his own. Then he gently lift-
er in his arms and carefully placed her back
d. Reluctantly pulling his clothes on, he blew
a kiss, then slipped back out the door.

he following morning, the prince and his par-
were sitting at the breakfast table when

He curled his body against her
the base of her neck. They had se
from the king and queen, but wh
alone, the prince had fondled a
princess until they could hardly
wedding night.

"Mmmm," Amanda purred as
awake. "Is this a beautiful dream

"No, my love," Mark said. "I
you tonight." He pressed his
Amanda's beautiful soft buttock
how much I want you."

"I want you, too," Amanda
should wait until we're wed."

"I can't wait any longer. I wan
he said, pausing, "I want to se
make love."

"But it's almost completely o
we dare not light a lamp. Somec
glow and come in."

He climbed from the bed and
to her feet. Quickly, he pulled he
her body and lifted her in his ar
you here, on the hearth, where
your eyes while I take you."

Amanda wrapped her arms
neck and kissed his smooth ches

I w
soo

T
bod
way
wit
bit
on
gen
len
his
me

sho
cha
lifte
of t
and
crie

Pri
Am
ed
in b
her

ent

Princess Amanda walked in. "How did you sleep?" the queen asked.

"I slept well," Amanda said, seating herself at the huge table. Then she turned and winked so only the prince could see. "But my back is a bit sore."

"Mother," the prince said, "isn't it time we began preparing for the wedding?"

"Immediately," the queen agreed.

Later that afternoon, the king found his wife in the garden. "All right," he said, seating himself next to her. "What was that final-test nonsense? I never heard of the test of vulnerability."

"Neither did I," the queen said. "It was really a test for our son. I knew he would never break his word and tell her about the pebble. I just wanted to see whether his love for her was great enough for him to figure out how to get what he wanted." The queen grinned slyly. "And, like father like son, he obviously did."

# The Spirit Voice

Hans, the farmer, and his wife, Meg, had been married for exactly twenty-five years that very day. In the beginning, everything had been wonderful and their life together had been exactly what they both wanted. Then there were children and so many other concerns that their bedroom play had dwindled to almost nothing. Now their children were grown and married, but their bed play hadn't improved.

Late that warm summer afternoon, the farmer had just finished milking the last of his cows when he heard a voice. "Oh, farmer," the soft, muffled voice said, "I am the voice of your guardian spirit. Take your wife to the forest clearing beside the waterfall and I will grant you a night of bliss."

"Why do you do this for me?" Hans asked.

"You've been a good and kind man ever since you first moved to this farm. You've taken only enough milk for your family to drink, only enough eggs to eat, and only enough wool for your wife to make into the garments she sells in the village. I've been watching you, and I now feel that you and your lovely wife deserve a reward."

"How will you make this happen?" the farmer asked.

"Go to the clearing and I'll tell you and your wife exactly what to do to regain the joys of your youth."

"But . . ."

"Stop asking so many questions," the voice said, "and take a blanket to the clearing tonight one hour after sundown."

The farmer rushed into the house and told his wife what had happened. It took only a little convincing for her to agree. An hour after sundown, the couple stood in the center of the clearing, the blanket laid at their feet.

"What shall we do?" Meg asked.

"Take off all your clothes," a soft voice said.

"That's the voice I heard," Hans said. He looked at his wife by the light of the almost-full moon and shrugged. After only a moment's hesitation, Hans sat on the blanket and watched as Meg began to remove her clothes. As she slowly unbuttoned her blouse, the farmer said, "I'd forgotten what a joy it is to watch you undress."

"I'd forgotten how good it is to see that look in your eyes." Slowly, she opened her blouse and revealed her tawny breasts, which were tipped with dark, smoky nipples.

As Hans reached out to touch her, the voice said, "Don't touch. Just look."

Smiling in the moonlight, Meg allowed the blouse to slip from her shoulders and untied the sash of her skirt. Soon she stood in the grass of the clearing naked. Hans's eyes roamed over her lush body, from her soft shoulders and long legs to the black triangle between her thighs. "So lovely," he whispered. "I'd forgotten."

"Now, farmer," the voice said. "Remove your clothes. Slowly, as your wife did."

Soon, the farmer's shirt and pants, shoes and socks joined his wife's clothes. "Now," the voice continued, "kneel on the blanket, facing each other, and close your eyes." When they had done as the voice asked, it said, "Touch each other with only your fingertips. Nothing more."

While Hans slowly ran his fingers over Meg's shoulders and down her arms, Meg tangled her fingers in her husband's chest hair, remembering its coarseness. They felt each other's eyes and lips. For long minutes, twenty fingers glided over skin smooth and rough, soft and hard, moist and dry.

Eyes still closed, Hans slid his hand down Meg's belly to the curly hair between her thighs. Meg caressed Hans's hip and slowly slid toward his hardened shaft. As Hans's fingers found Meg's moist, receptive opening, her hand stroked his hard erection. Together, with increasingly hungry fingers, the couple stroked and rubbed, waiting for the voice to tell them to go further.

"You may open your eyes and use your hands," the voice said, "but nothing more."

Meg parted her knees so Hans could slip two fingers into her hot, dripping pussy. Trembling with excitement, she wrapped her hand around his rock-hard cock and squeezed. They played and teased and excited each other until they could wait no longer. "I can't wait for the voice," Meg whispered.

"Nor can I," Hans growled. He pushed his wife onto her back and plunged into her, fucking her hard and fast until, with screams of pleasure, they both climaxed. Holding each other, the two lovers fell into a light sleep.

After that magic night, Hans and Meg went to the clearing often. Each time, the spirit voice found a new way for the two lovers to enjoy each other.

In the years that followed, their friends in the village often asked them the secret of their happiness. "We enjoy going to the clearing near the waterfall in the evenings." Then they would smile and wink at each other. "You'd be surprised how refreshing it can be."

# The Village Outcast

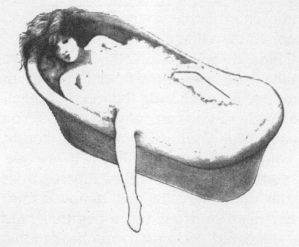

Every woman in the small village hated Marcella. She was young and pretty, and the local men constantly ogled her lush body, which was only partly hidden in the revealing peasant blouse she usually wore. The women knew that several of the unmarried men visited her tiny house late in the evenings. They suspected that a few of the married ones did, too.

One morning, when all the men were out in the fields, the women made their way silently into Marcella's hut, tied her hands, put a sack over her head, and dumped her into a wagon filled with straw. A fat old matron named Hilda drove her out of town and deep into the nearby woods. Farther and farther she drove, until there was little chance that Marcella would find her way back to the village.

As Hilda dumped Marcella from the wagon, she said, "Here's enough food for three days." She dropped a sack beside the road. "And there's a knife inside so you can cut your bonds. You will eventually find your way from the woods, but don't come back to our village. If we see you again, your punishment will be much worse."

By the time Marcella had removed the sack from her head and cut the ropes that held her hands, she could no longer even hear the wagon that had brought her. She stood up, dusted off her skirt, and then, having no plan, she picked up the food sack and wandered aimlessly through the thick woods.

Sometime during the afternoon of the third day, Marcella heard shots. Someone's out there, she thought. She started to cry for help, then stopped. It could be anyone, good or bad. Then she shook her head, because it really didn't matter. She hadn't seen a road or any sign of civilization for three days, and she was running out of food. She looked down at herself, straightened her blouse, dusted off her skirt, and pinched some color into her cheeks. "I'll be all right. I'll make out." She took a deep breath. "Help! Help me," she screamed.

"Where are you?" a male voice called.

"Here, right here." Marcella heard the sound of heavy feet crashing through the thick foliage. Suddenly, two men emerged from the undergrowth. Both were tall and bearded, and they wore soft brown shirts, matching leather jerkins, and tight leather pants. Not bad, she thought, looking the two men over. Not bad at all. "Oh, I'm so glad you found me. I'm totally lost." She arranged her face in a pleasing pout.

"Lost?" the taller one said. "You certainly are. You're many miles from the nearest road. The only thing around here is our cabin."

"Cabin." She sighed, untangling her long, soft hair with her fingers. "I had to sleep in a cave last night and I haven't been able to wash or anything." She smiled her most engaging smile.

"My name is Theron and this is my brother Bruno," the taller man said. "We're hunters and we shoot game in this forest."

"How do you do," she said. "I'm Marcella."

"You're very beautiful," Bruno said, his eyes roaming the girl's body.

"Thank you, Bruno. You know, I'd give any-thing for a drink of cool water and a tub to wash in." She winked. "And I do mean *anything*."

"Well," Theron said, "it's only a short walk to our cabin. I'm sure we can find a drink for you, and a washtub." Together, they made their way to a small but pleasant log cabin. Behind the build-ing was a small vegetable garden, and there were flowers beside the front door. As he saw her look-ing at the garden, Bruno said shyly, "I love things that grow."

Marcella stared at the obvious swelling between Bruno's legs. "I'll just bet you do." She followed the two handsome men into the spa-cious cabin. Theron handed her a cup of cool water and she drank every drop. As she put the cup on the table, she asked, "Do you really have a tub in which I might bathe?"

Theron and Bruno brought a giant washtub from behind the house, then filled it with hot water from a caldron near the fire. "I've even got some soft soap here," Theron said, handing a small cake to Marcella. He paused, then said, "We'll wait outside."

"You don't have to," Marcella said, smiling. "Wouldn't you like to watch? As a matter of fact, wouldn't you like to wash with me?"

Theron thought a moment, then pulled his jerkin and shirt off. "We certainly would."

While Marcella watched, Bruno also stripped to the waist. "Oh my," she purred, "you are both wonderful to look at." Slowly, she pulled her blouse over her head, exposing her large, firm breasts. Two sets of eyes were riveted on her smooth skin and tightly puckered nipples. Marcella untied her sash and allowed her skirt and pantaloons to fall to the floor. Stepping out of her shoes, she quickly climbed into the steaming water, and while the brothers watched, she thoroughly washed her body, caressing every inch of her skin with soapy hands.

"You know, I could use a wash, too," Theron said, scooping up a handful of soapy water and pouring it over his head. Rivulets of water ran over his heavily furred chest and down his belly.

"So could your brother," Marcella said, splashing water at the other half-naked man. Soon the brothers were soaked, as was the floor of the cabin. "Why don't you step out of those sopping pants," she said.

"Of course," Theron said, pulling off his soggy pants. Bruno followed his brother's lead and removed his trousers.

Marcella stood up in the tub, water sluicing

down her lush body. "Would you like to help me dry off?" When Theron handed her a towel, she said softly, "I had something else in mind. I thought you might dry me off with your mouths."

With no hesitation, Theron stuck out his tongue and licked droplets of water from Marcella's left breast while Bruno did the same with her right.

Marcella felt her knees begin to buckle as she relished the sensation of two mouths sucking at her breasts. Letting her head fall back, she tangled her fingers in each man's hair, pulling each head more tightly against her. "Oh yes," she moaned.

"You taste very good," Theron groaned, standing up.

"Very good indeed," Bruno echoed.

Marcella soaped her hands and took one heavy, swollen cock in each, rubbing slippery soap over the rock-hard erections. "Oh my, you are both so big." She stroked and squeezed until she knew they were ready to come. Quickly, she poured water over the two men, then knelt down in the tub. She pulled Theron until he stood in the tub in front of her. As she took his hard cock into her mouth, she guided Bruno's cock into her pussy from behind. With one cock filling her mouth and one filling her cunt, Marcella was in heaven.

All too soon, Theron's cock filled her mouth with come, and Bruno's spurted into her pussy. The men withdrew, and at her urging, Theron stroked her taut nipples and Bruno rubbed her clit with the tip of his now-deflating cock. Soon she screamed, "Yes. Like that. Don't stop." Her back arched and she climaxed, still kneeling in the tub.

Later, after dinner, Theron said, "We'd like you to live here with us. We have more than enough food, and we could make one another very happy. Would you stay?"

"Well," Marcella said, "I was trying to get back to my village."

"Is there anything that anyone in your village can offer you that we can't?" asked Theron.

"And don't forget," Bruno added, "every pleasure we offer here is double what you'd get anywhere else."

Marcella looked at the two brawny men eager to serve her, and after about a half of a second's thought, she opened her arms to the brothers. "After all," she conceded, "it's an offer no lusty woman in her right mind could refuse."

# Golden Locks

Odile had the longest, most beautiful hair in the village, and she knew it. She spent hours in the sun in front of her father's butcher shop combing the golden curls that hung almost to her knees, dreaming of the man she would one day marry.

One afternoon, her father sat down beside her, knowing he could put this moment off no longer. "Odile," he said hesitantly, "I've found a husband for you. His name is Galard and he's a wealthy landowner from the far side of the mountains. He's sending a coach for you tomorrow. You'll drive to his mansion and be married immediately."

Odile was silent for a long time. "Is he handsome?" she asked.

"He's very handsome, very rich, and only a few years older than you are. He heard of your beauty and sent an emissary to make all the arrangements." He cleared his throat. "And he wants many children."

Odile thought of all the servants and all the beautiful dresses she would have. And chocolates. She looked at her father's stained apron and smiled. And she'd never have to smell meat again. "What time will the coach be here?"

The following morning, in a whirlwind of activity, Odile left the village. She arrived at the enormous mansion and was whisked into the dimly lit chapel for a brief marriage ceremony. As she was hustled up to the bedroom, she realized that she had hardly seen her new husband. A serving girl quickly removed her gown and undergarments.

"Such wondrous hair." The girl sighed. As she picked up a comb, Odile sat up and took it from her hands. "No one touches my hair but me," she said, running the teeth of the comb through a long golden lock. "You may go." Modestly, she pulled her hair forward until it covered her naked breasts.

Moments after the serving girl departed, the bedroom door opened and her new husband walked in. "Magnificent," he said. "When I heard about your luxurious hair, I knew I had to have you." He sat down on the edge of the bed and twisted one curl around his fingers.

Odile slapped his hand away. "No one touches my hair but me."

"You're my wife now," Galard said as he stood up and removed his shirt. Odile continued to comb her hair, all the time watching the play of steel-hard muscles beneath his suntanned skin. As he pulled off his pants, the comb froze in Odile's curls. His body was white where his breeches hid his skin from the sun, and, from a nest of black curls between his thighs, his erection thrust forward, eager for her. As she watched him approach, Odile felt molten heat flow through her bloodstream and settle in a fiery caldron in her belly.

Galard sat on the edge of the bed and lifted a lock of hair. He used the end as a brush to caress her neck and shoulders. "You will love what I can do with this hair," he purred, brushing one erect nipple. He pressed her back onto the pillows and, without touching her in any other way, drew the soft lock of hair across the hollow of her belly. No area of her skin was untouched as Galard slid the silky strands over her body.

Odile's body was on fire as her hair glided across the backs of her knees and the sensitive skin of her thighs. Galard took one long lock from each side of her forehead and brushed the warm strands over his face. Then he pulled one lock down each side of her body, outside her tight breasts and then between her legs. He threaded one lock behind each thigh so that, when he pulled, her breasts were forced together and the lips of her pussy were pulled open. He buried his face in the valley of her bosom, licking and kissing her deep cleavage. He kissed a line down her belly and drove his tongue into her naval.

Odile's entire body was trembling as he pulled the hair taut, opening her further so his tongue could lick her most intimate flesh. "Tell me," he whispered as he flicked his tongue across her clit.

"Yes," was all she could say.

He positioned his body above her and, still using her hair to hold her wide open, slid his hard cock into her heat. He released her hair and, ever so slowly, drew the strands from between her legs and across her clit.

"Yes," she said again. "Yes." Lying in a golden pool of her hair, Galard and Odile twisted, bucked, and drove until they both climaxed. "Oh, my lord," she gasped. "I never imagined it would be so amazing."

Later, she stretched, catlike, enjoying the feel of Galard's body pressed against her. As she extended her arms above her, Galard wrapped a cord of her hair around her wrists, tying her arms together. "This hair of yours is going to provide many pleasures in the future."

Not moving her deliciously imprisoned wrists, Odile smiled and asked, "Do we have to wait for the future?"

# The Enchanted Prince

Prince John drove his hard cock into the woman's warm pussy and climaxed almost immediately. He withdrew and pecked a light kiss on her lips.

"All right, buster," the woman snapped, "that's it! I heard about you from several women, but I couldn't believe it until I spent these"—she raised an eyebrow—"very few minutes with you."

Smug and satisfied, the prince rolled onto his back and yawned. "Wasn't it good for you?"

"It was not, and you know it, you egotistical 'slam bam thank you, ma'am' popinjay."

"Now don't get all mad," he said, standing and pulling on his shirt. "Consider yourself lucky. You've been made love to by the best."

"Oh, I'm mad all right, and you're in deep trouble. You may think you're the best, but you're the worst, the most self-centered lover I've ever had." Suddenly, a magic wand appeared in her hand. "From now on, no intercourse for you until an innocent woman asks—no begs—for it." She tapped him on the shoulder with her wand and a tight leather restraint suddenly wound itself around his cock and balls, then around his waist.

"Now wait a minute," John said, unsuccessfully trying to loosen the leather around his loins. "Who the hell are you?"

"I'm a witch. I'm usually a good and loving witch, as a matter of fact. But there are limits."

Unable to remove his leather restraint, John pulled on his britches and smoothed the fabric over it. "What do I have to do to get this thing off?" he asked, now both annoyed and nervous.

"Here's how this will work. You must find a woman who knows nothing about your enchantment, a woman you truly want to pleasure. Then you just make love with her."

The prince smiled. "That doesn't seem difficult."

The witch smiled, as well. "It must be long, slow love to give her pleasure, with no intercourse. You must go gently, helping her to enjoy every step. Only when she is so excited by your loving that she begs you to enter her will your body be free of the spell. And, of course, once you are free, you will be free forever." The woman patted the leather that stretched tightly across his cock, then disappeared.

Over the next months, the prince tried lovemaking with several of the willing wenches in the local taverns, but to no avail. At the moment of truth the leather restraint remained in place. Finally, annoyed and thoughtful, John loaded a knapsack with food, wandered into the woods, and spent several days in a cave, deep in contemplation.

The pretty village girl with ebony black skin and flashing black eyes came to the glade near the cave one afternoon. Knowing nothing of the spell, she spread her blanket and relaxed in the warm sun. Accepting what he had to do, the prince wandered over and offered her some bread and cheese from his knapsack. They talked and promised to meet the following afternoon. Each day for the next week, the prince settled on the blanket next to her. Finally, one afternoon as she dozed, he murmured, "You know, you're very beautiful, Belinda."

"Thank you," she said, appreciating the man's almost irresistibly handsome face and sexy body. She had wanted him for days and hoped that maybe today...

John stroked her lips with the pad of his thumb, then leaned down and whispered in her ear. "I desire you so much."

She felt tiny kisses on her face and throat, burning everywhere they touched. "Yes. Oh yes."

He devoured her mouth, unable to get enough of her, moving his head, changing his position to better give her pleasure. Restraining his need to ravish her, John kissed and sucked each fingertip, then did the same with her toes. As he kissed her legs, she felt her dress and underwear slip off. She trembled as liquid heat flowed from her aching nipples to the empty place between her legs.

John's lips and tongue teased, advancing up her belly, then retreating until she was mindless with wanting. When she could wait no longer, Belinda tangled one hand in his hair and pulled his mouth to her breast. Her entire body shook with relief when he suckled, and it trembled as his hands traced the inside of her thigh, moving toward the heat that radiated so strongly from the center of her hunger.

Slowly, he told himself. Give her pleasure. John pinched and pulled at Belinda's nipples with one hand and pulled off his shirt with the other. He stretched out so his chest pressed against hers, rubbing his sweat-slick skin against her sensitive nipples. His foot made a path from ankle to knee; his hands roamed her arms, her ribs, her breasts and teased her soaked pussy. "God," he said, "you feel so good. I love touching and kissing you." And suddenly, he understood that it felt as wonderful to give pleasure as to get it. "I love pleasuring you."

"I want you," Belinda whispered. "I want you to make love to me." She took a deep shuddering breath. "Please!"

John pulled off his britches, and suddenly the leather restraint fell from his body. He used his knee to part the girl's thighs, and when he knew she could wait no longer, he positioned himself above her.

She was so excited that her body almost pulled him until he was sheathed entirely inside her. He looked into her eyes and knew it was as beautiful for her as it was for him. Slowly he began to move, establishing a rhythm that made them both satisfied and hungry at the same time.

Higher and higher they flew, until there was nowhere else to fly. She reached the sun and exploded with the heat of it, waves of pleasure washing over her. He shared her climax and let himself fly with her. For long moments, there was nothing but heat and swirling colors and the music of love. "Oh yes," she moaned. "So good."

"Yes, it was," he said softly.

"Will you be here tomorrow?" she whispered.

He could go home and resume his life, he realized. But as he stroked Belinda's soft ebony breasts, he knew that all he wanted was to be here with his wonderful lover. "Oh yes, my love," he said. "You will see me often and we will make love. And I hope you will teach me how to give you more pleasure."

"We will find all the pleasures there are," she said as she cuddled against John's naked body, and, in the light of the setting sun, they both fell asleep.

# The Magic Melody

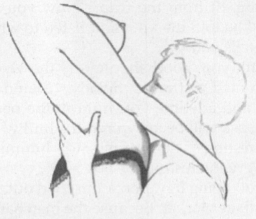

For weeks, Benjamin, a shepherd, had been try-ing to trap the fox who had been terrorizing his sheep. One morning when he went to check his trap, he found a not-yet-full-grown kit inside and a fully grown vixen beside it. "I'm so sorry that my son has been terrorizing your sheep," the vixen said. "If you let him go, I promise that I'll teach him good manners."

"But my sheep are so skittish now that it's extra work for me to keep them from straying," Benjamin said.

"I'll give you a reward if you let my little one go."

Benjamin took the vixen's word and released the young kit from the trap. "Now you learn to behave," he told the kit, "and listen to what your mother tells you."

"Thank you, good shepherd," the vixen said. She hummed a strange melody. "Memorize this melody and anytime you hum it, the next question you ask will be answered truthfully."

"Interesting," Benjamin said, humming the tune. "Very interesting."

The following day, Benjamin tried out the tune at the village market. Because the merchants were forced to be honest about prices and values, he got a surprisingly large sum for the wool he was selling and got a good bargain on his groceries. As he walked home with food for the week in his sack, he thought about his wife. She had always been very shy and reserved, and he wondered whether the tune might help him find out more about her, particularly in the bedroom.

That evening, after dinner, he sat beside his wife in the main room of their cottage with some new wine he had bought. He draped his arm around her shoulder and whispered in her ear. "Darling, what would you like to do this night?"

"Whatever you would like," his wife said.

Benjamin hummed his magic melody, then asked again, "What would you really like to do?"

She laid her head back on his arm and said, "I'd like you to kiss me." She pointed to her lips. "Here."

He kissed her lips, licking and nibbling at her mouth. He swirled his tongue with hers and inhaled her soft, clean scent. He hummed, then asked, "Now what?"

"I'd like to feel your hands on my breasts," she answered. She pulled her blouse off over her head so her husband could stroke her soft, smooth flesh. Humming softly, Benjamin teased, swirling his fingers close to, but not touching, his wife's nipples. "Pinch them," she said, groaning. "Make me feel your fingers."

He squeezed and pulled at her nipples, watching them get hard and pointed. Her breasts seemed to swell and beckon. "Shall I suck them?" he asked.

"Yes," she whispered. "Suck them hard. Make them hurt."

Benjamin was surprised at her answer. He never imagined that his wife might enjoy a bit of pain. He hummed, then asked again.

"Yes," she answered. "Make them hurt."

Benjamin used his teeth and bit her tender flesh. "Yes," she moaned. "That feels so good." She grabbed the back of his neck and arched her back, forcing herself against his face. "More," she begged.

Benjamin sucked and pulled at her tits until her nipples were larger and tighter than he had ever seen them. Humming his magic melody, he asked, "Now what?"

"Be a little rough with me. Rip off my clothes and fuck me hard, right here on this floor."

Again, Benjamin was amazed. He always tried to be gentle and slow, loving and tender. But with the help of his melody, he knew that his wife wanted him to act differently right now—hard and fast. He wrapped his wife's hair around his fist and pulled, forcing her head back. "Like this?" he asked.

"Yes. Do it!"

He grabbed the front of her skirt and pulled it off her body. Then he ripped her pantalets down the front and, tugging at his britches, pushed her onto the rug. He slid his hands between her legs and felt the slick moisture that flowed from her excited body. One last time, he hummed and asked, "Are you sure?"

"Fuck me good!" she yelled.

Still partially dressed, Benjamin plunged into her overheated body and drove into her hard, thrusting over and over. "Yes," she screamed. "Harder." She grabbed his buttocks and bucked. "Yes, yes, yes! Don't stop!" She grabbed his hand and slid it between their bodies. "Rub here," she said, pushing his finger against her erect clit.

As his wife screamed and climaxed, Benjamin came, spurting deep into her body. They lay, panting, for many minutes.

"I don't know what got into me tonight," his wife said after she'd calmed down.

Smiling to himself, Benjamin said, "I don't, either." As he lay tangled with his wife, Benjamin thought about the things he wanted to tell her about their lovemaking, secret fantasies he wanted to share with her. Maybe, he told himself, maybe I'll teach her the magic melody and then I, too, will be "forced" to reveal my deepest, darkest desires.

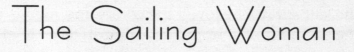

# The Sailing Woman

Daria was the daughter of a sailing man and lived in a tiny hut only a hundred yards from the great sea. For months at a time, her father and brothers would sail the seas, ferrying rich cargoes from foreign land to foreign land. Then they would come home and tell Daria and her mother wonderful stories of all the exotic places they had visited.

When she was about nine, Daria had been allowed to sail as far as the nearby port, then back, and she had fallen in love with the sea. She loved the ocean waves and the feel and smell of the salt spray. She loved the colors and moods of the sea and sky from the calmest days to the fiercest storms. As she grew, all she ever wanted to be was a sailor. "Why can't I go along?" Daria pleaded. "I want to sail the seas and visit wonderful faraway places."

"You're a foolish girl," her mother had said just that very morning. "You can't be a sailor. You're a woman and one day soon you will marry. You will keep house for your sailor husband. You will cook and clean. You will share his bed, bear and raise his children. That is your destiny."

"But Mother," Daria said, "I don't want to be left behind to do housework. I want to travel everywhere there is to go, see everything there is to see."

"You are a foolish girl," her mother said, "and I'll hear no more about it."

"Your mother's right," her father said. He had just come home and was leaving again the following day. "And what's more, it's getting to be time for you to choose a husband. There are several young men in the village who have asked me about you."

"Never," Daria proclaimed. "I won't marry and become someone's wife and be land-bound forever." She stormed out of the house and ran to the tip of the rocky point where the waves from the great sea broke and sea spray washed the giant rocks. There she sat for a long time, staring at the line where the sea met the sky.

Suddenly, someone leapt from the water and landed at her side. Daria stared. The lower half of his body was fishlike, with a heavy tail and fins. The upper half of his body was all man, with muscular chest and well-developed arms. His face was strong and angular, and he had long black hair that hung down to his shoulders. Water poured from him as he settled on the rock.

As Daria watched, he extended his arms to the sea. "Neptune," he cried over the pounding of the waves, "it is I." Then he whistled and made several sounds Daria had never heard before. Slowly, as Daria stared, his bright blue and yellow fish scales began to fall off, his tail began to divide, and his cock appeared between a pair of tightly muscled legs. "Good day to you," the man said, unconcerned that he lay next to Daria completely naked. He brushed water from his body with his long fingers.

"G-g-g-good day to y-y-you, too," the girl stammered, unable to take her eyes from his beautiful form. "Who are you?"

"My true name would be impossible for you to pronounce, but you may call me Garal."

"What are you doing here"—she gestured toward his naked body—"like that?"

"Like what?" the man said.

"You have no clothes on," the girl said.

"The better to swim in the great sea," he said. "Come, swim with me."

"I cannot," Daria said.

Garal stood up and, with a whisk of his hand, pulled Daria's simple dress over her head, leaving her standing naked in the salt spray. "Of course you can. Follow me." And with that, he dove into the foaming sea.

Daria hesitated only a moment, then followed Garal into the water. As she swam, she felt Garal's smooth body sliding over her skin, his hips brushing her back and sides. Like a porpoise, he dove and circled, rubbing his chest, sides, and legs against her. The feeling was heavenly, wet skin against wet skin. Soon, Daria learned to anticipate where he would surface next and moved her body so he would rub across her breasts and belly. As he circled, she ran her hands over his smooth, hairless body.

In one movement, he came up, with his back between her legs, and lifted her almost completely out of the water. "Ride me, sweet one. Ride on my back."

Daria wrapped her legs around his waist and together they made their way into deeper water. Almost out of sight of land, she felt Garal turn under her. He looked at her breasts, then into her eyes, and smiled. Slowly, his hands circled her waist, then slid up her ribs until his fingers tweaked her puckered nipples. "You're very beautiful," he whispered, caressing her flesh as her legs encircled his chest, her flanks flexing against his ribs.

Daria wasn't a stranger to love play, but this was different from anything she had ever done with the boys of the village. She was floating, bobbing, drifting in the cool water, with Garal's warm hands everywhere. When she thought she would sink, Garal tightened his hold on her waist and slid his chest back and forth between her thighs. His skin pressed the swollen flesh of her sex, her slippery juices mingling with the seawater.

With Daria's legs still wrapped around his body, Garal maneuvered until his great cock was poised at the mouth of her sheath. "Tell me you want me," he said over the roar of the waves.

Overcome with the beauty of her feelings, Daria said, "Oh yes. Do it. Join with me."

Garal held her partway out of the water, then lowered her onto his staff. Their buoyancy adding to the feelings of ecstasy, the two lovers joined and rolled. "Don't stop," Daria yelled over and over.

"Never, my love. I will never stop."

Hands, mouths, and bodies rubbed and pounded until Garal and Daria climaxed together.

Floating on the swells, they caught their breath. "Oh, Garal," Daria gasped, "that was fantastic." Then her face became sad. "But what of us? We can never be together."

"But we can, my love. I know your longing to be part of the sea and I can promise you that if you choose to live with me, your life will be filled with adventure, amorous and otherwise. Is that what you want?"

Without a moment's hesitation, Daria nodded.

Garal slid his hands down Daria's flanks and, to her amazement, her legs fused and slowly became covered with iridescent green scales. She watched as his body re-formed also.

"Oh Garal, how wonderful." With her lover following, Daria dove gracefully through a great wave and swam toward the horizon.

She never looked back.

# The Duke and the Lady

Veronica had been riding across her father's vast estate when a dozen men galloped from the forest and surrounded her mount. "Don't make a fuss," one said, "and we won't hurt you. The duke wants you unharmed."

Quickly, she was pushed into a carriage and, surrounded by the horses and men, driven away. Fortunately, since she was well treated, the journey wasn't any more uncomfortable than it had to be. They stopped often and slept each night at a carefully selected inn along the road.

After more than a week, they arrived at a palatial mansion high on a hill. She was hustled from the carriage, up an enormous spiral staircase, and into a richly appointed bedroom. When she heard someone lock the door behind her, she became afraid. For hours, she paced the room, waiting for the mysterious duke to tell her what this was all about.

It seemed forever. The light from the window had long since faded and the tray of food someone had brought lay undisturbed on a table. Finally, the door opened and Veronica saw the uncommonly handsome man who had ordered her to be brought here. He stood, framed in the opening, his soft white shirt and brown leather jacket showing off his well-developed chest, his tight fawn-colored riding pants barely concealing his heavily muscled thighs. Although she was frightened of him, Veronica also yearned to run her fingers through his long black hair and feel its softness. But his piercing blue eyes prevented her from moving.

"You're mine now, darling," he said, his voice soft and mellow, "and I won't hurt you. You're a precious jewel to be worshiped and loved, and I intend to do both."

As Princess Veronica clutched her lace shawl across her breasts, her hands trembled. But she knew that, although she had never been with a man before, it wasn't fear. It was desire, hot and liquid, and it flowed through her body like honey. She had never felt anything like this.

Slowly, he crossed the small room and stood so close to her that she could feel his breath against her face. He raised his hand and stroked her cheek with the side of his thumb. "So soft," he whispered. "Your skin is like warm cream. Is it that soft all over?"

She was silent, unable to speak, fully under the man's spell. "I kidnapped you to convince you that we belong together. Let me show you. Let me love you," he whispered, sliding his fingers down her slender neck. She watched his lips move, watched the light from the candles on the desk reflect in his midnight blue eyes.

"I know you are still untouched and I promise that I won't do anything you don't want. Tell me to stop at any point and I will." He hesitated, waiting for her reaction.

She realized that she didn't want to stop him. She wanted him more than she had ever wanted anything. She wanted him now, here, in his bedroom.

When she remained silent, he murmured, "Oh yes, love. Oh yes." He placed his index finger under her chin and lifted her face. Softly, he brushed his lips across hers, gently, like the wing of a butterfly.

The princess closed her eyes as his lips tasted hers. She should resist, she thought, but she couldn't pretend. She wanted him and knew that she would let him do anything he wanted. As the duke cupped her face in his palms, she let her body melt against his, feeling the hardness of his chest and the bulge below that pressed against her belly. Some yearning deep inside of her made her press her hips closer, letting him know her hunger.

She lifted her hands and placed her palms flat against his chest. She could feel the heat of his body through his shirt, but she wanted to be closer. Impatiently, she dragged his jacket from his broad shoulders, pulled his shirt free from his pants, and slid her hands underneath. His chest was covered with soft hair and she greedily ran her fingers through it while the duke devoured her mouth, his tongue sliding in and out with a rhythm that was echoed in her belly.

It took only moments for them to be naked on his wide silken bed. "So beautiful," he purred, gazing at her luscious breasts and narrow waist. With a featherlight touch, his fingers traced across her jaw, down her neck, and out to the point of her shoulder.

It wasn't enough for Veronica. She wanted so much more. She took his hand and pressed it against the soft flesh of her breast. His caress caused her nipple to contract. He licked at her lips with long, sensuous strokes, then slid the flat of his tongue across the pulse in her throat to her swollen breast. He blew a stream of cool air along the damp path, causing heat to slash deep to her core. She could feel her own wetness on her thigh.

As his lips nursed at her breast, his hand slid down to fondle her swollen flesh, his fingers sliding through her warmth. Wanting to touch him also, the princess slid her hand down his chest. When she hesitated at his navel, unsure whether to continue, he groaned, "Don't be shy, my dove. Touch me. I will die without your touch." He took her hand and stroked the palm with the tip of his hard shaft. "Hold me," he moaned.

"Oh yes, my love," she whispered as she wrapped her hand around his hard shaft. Velvet over iron, she thought, and, no longer reluctant, she pressed him toward her virgin opening. Despite a moment's pain when they joined, she reveled in the feel of his cock as it filled her completely. Over and over, he drove into her, until she was soaring. They came then, together, waves of pleasure crashing over them until they both screamed their happiness.

Later, when they had calmed, he said, "Shall I take you back to your home, my love?"

"Never," she whispered. "My home is with you for as long as you want me."

"Forever, my darling. Forever."

# The Thirteenth Suitor

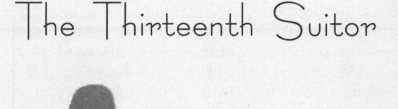

Princess Liana closed the door to the music room of the palace and heaved a great sigh. "If I have to meet one more overbearing, self-centered, egotistical prince who's only interested in my dowry, I'll scream." She dropped into a chair in the parlor and a serving maid handed her a cup of tea. "Twelve of them in the past week," she groaned, "and no one I would spend a long weekend with, much less the rest of my life." She smiled. This evening's candidate had even stripped off his shirt to let her touch his well-developed chest. "Oh God, save me."

But she knew that she would have to keep trying. Since her father had announced her availability for marriage, princes, dukes, earls, and other noblemen had been flocking to the palace for a chance to demonstrate how muscular, brave, beautiful, strong, wise, courteous, and generally wonderful they were. Each tried to convince her how lucky she would be should she choose him. And if she didn't select a fiancé within the next few days, her father would pick one for her.

The princess yawned, finished her tea, and wandered into her bedroom, stripping off her dress and petticoats as she walked. Three maids helped her off with the rest of her clothes and into her white cotton nightdress. "Good night, Your Highness," they said in unison, closing the door behind them.

"Peace and quiet." She sighed, settling into a soft chair by the fire.

"Don't scream," a soft voice said from a darkened corner. "I only want to talk to you."

Princess Liana took a deep breath. "How dare you enter my chamber without my permission?" She clasped her hands to keep them from trembling. "Take one step toward me and I'll scream."

"I pray you won't do that," the voice said. "I'm here to request your hand in marriage."

The princess relaxed a bit. "A novel approach," she said, "but why didn't you make an appointment with the chamberlain like everyone else?"

"I'm not like anyone else," he said. "I wanted some private time to help you understand how wonderful we would be together. I've loved you for a long time."

"Do I know you?"

"Not really. We've met several times, but you didn't notice me. I saw you, how beautiful and sensual you are. And I wanted you. I want a chance to convince you how good we would be together."

"Not a bad approach," she said, stretching her legs. "But how do you plan to do that? I can't even see you."

"You won't need to see me, just hear my words. I'm going to tell you about our wedding night. The wedding will be held in my castle by the river," he said, "and we'll be tired from all the festivities. We'll probably be carried up to my bedroom by some of the guests; then they'll close the door and we'll be alone."

"We will?"

"Close your eyes and see it," the voice said. "The room is cool, but the fire is warm, so we'll stand near it while I kiss you, long and sweet." He let out a long sigh. "I love your lips, so red and full."

"Mmm," the princess purred.

"While I kiss you, I'll take all the pins from your hair and run my fingers through it. Then I'll slowly undress you. First, I will see your beautiful breasts, glowing round and white in the light from the fire. The nipples will be firm and tight, begging for my mouth."

Without conscious thought, the princess closed her eyes and cupped her hands beneath her small, tight breasts.

"I will stroke your skin, then suckle at your breasts until you're groaning, wanting more."

"Then what?" the princess said, her voice breathy and hoarse.

"Then I'll remove my clothing and the clothing that covers the lower part of your body and caress your waist and back and buttocks. I'll knead your behind while I press your body against me and hold you while I nibble at your neck and shoulder. Can you feel it?"

"Yes," the princess purred, rubbing her breasts and pinching her nipples. "It feels so good."

"Take off that nightdress so you can feel everything so much better."

Without hesitation, she pulled off her night-dress and settled back into the chair.

"As we stand together on our wedding night, you're getting more and more anxious for me. You're aching deep in your belly and between your legs. You need me. Slide your fingers down your belly and show me where you need me."

Liana slid her hands down her stomach until her fingers touched her springy hair. "Farther," the voice whispered. "Touch where you need me on our wedding night."

Her fingers slid lower, across the wet, slippery flesh. "Rub it the way I will. Touch where it feels best." The princess rubbed and explored her body. Every place she touched satisfied but also created a deeper need. When she hesitated, the voice encouraged. "Don't stop. Keep touching the way I will. Learn the hunger you're capable of and the joy when that hunger is satisfied."

She stroked until she found a special spot that gave her the most pleasure. She kept stroking until the spasms that began in her pussy consumed her entire body. "Oh Lord," she moaned. "So good."

For many minutes, the room was silent. Then, as Princess Liana sat up, a vaguely familiar form walked from the shadows. He was very tall and very thin and not very good-looking at all. The princess didn't notice.

"That's not nearly as good as it would be like on our wedding night," the man said. He bowed. "Prince Michael, at your service."

"Not as it *would* be on our wedding night," the princess said. "As it *will* be."

# In the Forest

Once upon a time, in a peaceful kingdom near a great woods, lived a girl named Priscilla. Her father and two brothers went into the woods every day and returned with logs, which they sold in the nearby village. Priscilla and her mother stayed home and took care of the house, doing the cooking and cleaning. Fortunately, it wasn't a difficult job, so Priscilla had plenty of time to spend on more pleasant things. She often met men from the nearby village in a clearing in the woods, near a crystal stream, and frittered away the afternoon rolling naked with them in the soft grass or on the blanket she always had with her.

One afternoon, she arrived at the clearing. Nibbling on some wild berries, she heard a voice. "Help me. I'm stuck." She followed the voice and found a girl of about her age high up in a tree. "I can't get down," the girl said. "My dress is caught." Priscilla picked up a long branch and used it to unhook the stranger's dress from its entrapment.

"Thank you so much," the girl said as she climbed down from the tree. "I didn't think anyone would ever come."

"I'm just glad I heard you," Priscilla said. "But who are you and what in the world were you doing up there?"

"My name's Gilda and I'm from the other side of the village," the girl said. "I'm embarrassed to admit it, but I come here often, hoping to watch you with the men you meet."

"Spying?" Priscilla demanded.

"Yes," Gilda said wistfully. "I enjoy watching you and thinking how it would feel if it were me. With those men, I mean."

"You've never?"

"I'm to be married soon and if I went to my marriage bed already taken, it would be a disgrace. But I'm so curious."

Priscilla smiled. "I can help you understand what's to happen, yet leave you unspoiled."

"You can?" Gilda said. When Priscilla nodded, Gilda quickly agreed. "I know I must remove my clothes," she said, taking off her blouse. "I've seen you here so often and admired your beautiful skin. It looks like the finest satin." Quickly, the two women took off all their clothes.

Priscilla took Gilda's hand and kissed the tip of each finger. "Do you want to touch me?" she asked. She placed the girl's hand against her breast and felt Gilda's hand tremble. Despite her hesitancy, Gilda's hand moved as if on its own, fingers swirling and teasing. "You feel as soft as I had expected. May I kiss you?"

The two women kissed, drinking each other's sweetness. They collapsed onto the blanket and ran curious hands over each other's bodies. The curve of a back, the hollow of an underarm, the swell of a buttock—all were smoothed and stroked while their mouths learned about each other.

Priscilla guided Gilda's mouth to her tit, placing her nipple in the girl's mouth. "Taste it, Gilda. Taste my breast." Neither woman could keep her body still. Restless hunger possessed them both. When Priscilla could stand no more, she pressed Gilda onto her back on the blanket. Carefully, she parted the girl's legs and kissed the insides of her thighs.

As she kissed, she inhaled the womanly fragrance of her damp pussy. She's as hot and ready as I am, Priscilla said to herself. She touched her tongue to Gilda's swollen clit while she tickled Gilda's swollen labia with her fingers. As she licked and stroked, she felt Gilda's orgasm building. She lightly bit the tiny hard bud and heard Gilda cry out.

When Gilda's spasms passed, Priscilla climbed over the supine woman and crouched so her hot cunt was over the woman's face. "Do it to me as I did it to you," she said. "Then put your fingers into me."

Gilda gladly tasted the unfamiliar delicacy, using the pointed tip of her tongue to learn every crevice and fold of Priscilla's vagina. When she discovered the hard love button, she lashed her tongue over it, feeling the woman tremble.

As she licked, she probed the soaking, slippery opening with her finger, slowly sliding it into her partner's urgent body. "More," Priscilla cried, and Gilda inserted a second finger. Gilda instinctively knew the fucking motion and rhythmically inserted and withdrew her two fingers. When she added a third, she heard Priscilla scream, "Now.

Right now." Gilda's mouth was drenched in cream and her fingers felt the waves of Priscilla's orgasm as she came.

Later, as the two women lay together, Priscilla asked, "How often do you wander through my woods?"

"Once a week," Gilda answered.

"Well, if you tell me when you'll be here, sometimes we can do this and sometimes you can climb that tree and watch me pleasure one of the men of the village." Priscilla giggled. "I can already picture your wedding night. Won't your husband be surprised by how much a simple virgin can know."

# The Sea Sprite

Late one afternoon, a young man named Kedar was walking by the sea after dinner, thinking about how bored he was. He had lived his entire life here in the tiny fishing village on the edge of nowhere. "It's too quiet here!" he yelled out over the endless water. "Nothing exciting ever happens!" He smiled, thinking that soon he would have enough money saved to go to the city and have a real adventure.

Suddenly, seemingly out of nowhere, a beautiful girl appeared by his side. "Hello," she said, gazing straight into his eyes. "My name is"—she

hesitated, as if considering, then continued—
"Alexia. May I walk with you?"

They walked away from the village, toward a
deserted stretch of beach. For the next hour,
Alexia asked him the most unusual questions
about life and the people in the village and the
things he liked to do. As twilight approached,
they sat on the sand to watch the sun set.

The way Alexia kept looking at him was
driving him crazy. There was an open, childlike
curiosity about her. Her eyes were the color of
the sea, sort of green and sort of blue—no, he
couldn't describe their color any more than he
could describe the color of her hair. It was at
once red and gold, all the shades of the leaves in
autumn.

In the fading light, she took his hand, and as
she watched the sky darken, he watched her, his
heart hammering. God, he thought, she's so beautiful. As the minutes passed, it became almost
impossible to repress the mounting desire he was
feeling for her. But he knew he must. After all,
they had only just met.

"Can we do something else now?" Alexia
asked in her slightly throaty whisper.

Why don't we lie down on the sand so I can

tear all of your clothes off and ravish your magnificent body? he thought.

"That sounds nice," Alexia said.

"Huh?"

"Lying on the sand and making love." She looked at him and smiled. "It sounds like something I would enjoy very much."

He knew he hadn't said anything aloud, but then, several times before, it seemed that she had read his thoughts. He glanced over and saw Alexia's small breasts barely covered by the soft gauzy shirt she wore. Her nipples stood out through the lightweight fabric. She smiled at him and pulled him toward her as if she again knew what he was thinking.

"You may think I'm crazy, but sometimes it seems that you can read my thoughts. Can you?"

"Only the very strong ones," she admitted somewhat ruefully. When she saw his puzzled look, she continued. "I'm not from here. I'm from somewhere very far away." She gazed out over the darkening sea.

"Out there?" Kedar asked.

She nodded. "I came here to learn about men and women and how they interact." She bit her lower lip and lowered her lashes. "Every way in which they interact."

"Yeah, sure," he said, thinking that she must take him for a total idiot.

"No, really. And I don't think you're a total idiot." She grinned.

Nonplussed, Kedar continued. "Okay. Let's assume that you're not completely nuts and I'm not completely nuts. Let's assume that you mean what you're saying. Why me?"

"Absolutely no reason, except that you interested and attracted me from the first time I saw you walking along the beach many weeks ago. It took me a while to work out all the details, but once I did, I came here to find you."

Kedar stared straight ahead and tried not to think about her small, high, tight breasts with their large and erect nipples.

Alexia turned his face until he was looking at her. Then she brushed one fingertip over her nipple, making it pucker. As he stared, she said, "I can read your excitement and I can make it good for you. I know just what you want most."

Although Kedar was taken aback by her forwardness, he had to admit that she was right. He wanted her very badly. His cock was so rock-hard, it was almost painful.

"I don't like it that you're in pain," she said. "I can help." Through his pants, Alexia pressed the palm of her hand against his hard penis. "I can feel what you're feeling, and the sensations are wonderfully exciting."

Kedar groaned and let his head fall back.

"Oh," Alexia said, her eyes wide. "I didn't expect this to feel so soft yet so hard." She reached over, unfastened his pants, then wiggled a finger deep into the opening in the front. She slid the soft pad of her finger up and down Kedar's erection. "That feels wonderful," she said, panting. "And it's making you so excited. That excitement . . . I've never felt anything like it."

He could hardly catch his breath. "Are you actually feeling what I'm feeling?"

She shivered with pleasure. "Yes, yes. I can experience what you feel and I know exactly what you want." She pulled his cock out of his pants, until it stood firm in his lap. She licked her lips and kissed the tip, which was already oozing with thick fluid. When he reached for her, she said, "No. Just relax. I want to share your pleasure with you. Don't move; just feel."

Alexia wrapped her hand around Kedar's thick shaft and squeezed, pressing slightly downward, pulling the skin taut over the tip. "Oh my! That's wonderful," she said.

Kedar had no idea how she was doing it, but Alexia was touching him exactly the way he wanted to be touched. He didn't know whether she was inside his mind or not, but whatever it was, it was incredible. He pictured her mouth on his cock and suddenly felt her wet lips. "Oh yes. Do that. Take it all the way," he whispered.

Alexia drew Kedar's penis deep into her mouth, until the entire length was held within her wetness. She moved her tongue so it tasted every part of his shaft. She pulled back slowly. "Ah." She sighed. And, speaking with the tip of Kedar's cock against her lips, she murmured, "I never imagined how good this would feel."

"Me, either," Kedar said as Alexia sucked him into her mouth again. She knew precisely the correct rhythm of sucks and licks it would take to bring him to the peak of pleasure. Then, before he could climax, she backed off just a little, sharing the combination of torture and pleasure that Kedar was feeling. "Oh, Alexia," he groaned, "do it for me." He saw her smile.

"Like this?" She sucked his entire length into her mouth and reached into his pants to scratch his balls with her fingernail. He couldn't hold back, and he erupted into her mouth. As he came, he felt her body convulse with pleasure.

"Incredible," they said in unison.

More. I want more, Kedar thought to himself.

Alexia smiled knowingly. "And you shall have it," she whispered.

# The Talisman

Oh, fairy godmother," Lissande said, gazing into her dusty mirror, "you've given me such beautiful clothes to wear to the ball at the palace and I'm so grateful."

"Of course you are, my dear," the godmother said. "And you'll have a wonderful time, meet several eligible noblemen, and maybe even find your heart's desire."

"I'm nervous. Who will want to dance with me? I'm not beautiful or desirable."

The godmother looked at Lissande and shrugged her shoulders. The girl was magnificent, long golden hair, deep green eyes, and a face and figure beyond compare. "I've told you and told you: You're sensational. Your sisters have you convinced that you're ugly, but actually, they've always kept you hidden so you won't outshine them."

"So you've said, but I look at myself and I see an ordinary-looking woman with little to offer a nobleman."

The godmother shook her head, grabbed Lissande by the shoulders, and turned her around. Her voice soft and conspiratorial, she whispered, "I have a magic talisman for you. But you must close your eyes while I make it ready." Lissande closed her eyes and the godmother fumbled in her skirt pocket and pulled out an old silver chain. "It will make you desirable to all the men at the dance. They will see you as a gorgeous, sensual woman and will be swept away with desire."

Checking that her charge couldn't see, the godmother reached down, pulled the jeweled buckle from one of her shoes, and hung it from the chain. Quickly, she placed the chain around Lissande's neck. "Look at yourself now."

Lissande turned and looked into the mirror. The small jeweled square hung low, almost hidden within her generous cleavage. As she turned to examine her reflection, the godmother whispered, "You will attract men like honey attracts bees. They will want to kiss your soft, sweet lips and caress your delicate skin. You will be irresistible."

Lissande straightened and smoothed the fabric over her tiny waist and generous hips. An enigmatic smile played at the corners of her mouth. "You know, you're right. I can see the effect of the talisman already. I am better-looking."

The godmother pulled Lissande from the mirror and hustled her down the stairs to the waiting coach. "Have a wonderful time." At her signal, the coach drove into the night.

Lissande arrived at the palace ballroom and silently made her way to the punch bowl. Would the talisman work? she wondered as she sipped a glass of punch and watched the beautiful men and women twirl around the room.

"Hi, gorgeous," a voice behind her said. "I'm Lord DeMonde. Phillippe to you. Are you alone?"

Lissande started to walk away, then stopped herself. He could be the man of my dreams. She touched the talisman hanging between her breasts, then answered, "Not anymore."

"Dance with me." For an hour, they drifted around the floor, talking and laughing. As the music became slower, Phillippe held her closer. "You're a lovely and intoxicating woman," he whispered into her ear, nibbling at the lobe.

"I'm glad you think so," Lissande said, gazing into his dark brown eyes.

He danced her into a dimly lit corner and as they swayed to the music, he placed tiny kisses on the sensitive skin behind her ear. "So lovely and sexy." He nipped at the tendon at the side of her neck.

The charm was working, Lissande realized, and she'd never have a better chance to taste life's pleasures. "You are a very sexy man," she said hoarsely.

Without another word, Phillippe led Lissande into a small curtained alcove and pulled her against the length of his body. His lips captured hers and, for the first time, Lissande felt a man's yearning body pressed against her own. She opened her mouth and Phillippe's tongue invaded, stroking hers. As they kissed, his fingers explored the soft skin on her neck and shoulders.

Lissande slid her arms around his neck and clung, holding him close, trying to ease the sudden ache in her breasts and between her legs. "Oh, Phillippe," she whispered, her lips only a breath from his, "you feel so good." She moved so the curtain closed behind her, enveloping them in almost total darkness.

His lips still against hers, Phillippe caressed her collarbone and down the planes of her chest until his fingers slipped beneath the bodice of her gown and found the soft globe of her breast. As his fingers brushed the tip, Lissande's nipple tightened and her breast swelled until it filled his hand. She let her head fall back and floated in the sea of sensations. "More," she whispered.

Phillippe backed up until his calves touched the settee at the rear of the alcove. He picked Lissande up in his arms and sat, placing her gently in his lap. Quickly, he shifted the bodice of her gown until he could suckle at her hot, erect nipple. "Oh God, you taste so good," he whispered, pinching her other breast and, simultaneously, reaching for her ankle.

Lissande moved so he could caress the skin on her calves and the backs of her knees. As he brushed the delicate flesh at the inside of her thighs, she shivered, parting her legs to allow his fingers better access.

The full skirt and petticoats were no impediment to Phillippe's fingers, and he found her hot, sticky, swollen flesh, covered only by a thin layer of the finest fabric. "This silk is not half as soft as your skin," he whispered, his mouth moving from breast to breast. He gently bit the tip of one nipple and, as Lissande's body shuddered, he rubbed the swollen button of her clit. "So responsive," he said, rubbing her heat.

"Don't stop," she said, feeling the tension rise in her belly and the secret place between her legs. Higher and higher he drove her, until she reached her climax. As she was about to scream out her pleasure, Phillippe covered her mouth with his. He continued stroking until he had drawn every ounce of her orgasm from her.

Realizing that they had been gone from the ball for a long time, Phillippe said, "Go riding with me in my very private carriage first thing tomorrow morning." He smoothed her skirt and restored her bodice to its original location. Then he took her hand and placed it on the hard bulge in his trousers. "Please say you'll meet me."

"Of course I'll meet you," Lissande said as they slipped from the alcove. For propriety's sake, they separated and she danced with several other men, including a handsome blond count who invited her to go to the theater with him the following evening. I have found my heart's desire, she realized, agreeing to meet still another lord in the parlor later that evening.

As she sipped some punch, she reached for the talisman and realized that she hadn't felt it around her neck since her interlude in the alcove. Lissande looked, and she quickly found it under the settee. "When those other men found me attractive," she said aloud, "I wasn't wearing this. Maybe I really am beautiful and seductive, and that has always been my heart's desire." She giggled, slipped the buckle and chain into her pocket, and made her way back to the dance floor. She batted her eyelashes at a handsome lord and smiled behind her fan. I guess my fairy godmother was right, she thought as the lord crossed the room toward her. I have found my heart's desire.

# The Three Princesses

But sire, I did nothing," Lord Timothy said.

"You saved my son from the evil knight," the king said, "and you shall have the choice of one of my three daughters to wed. They are all well-bred princesses and any one of them will make you rich and happy."

"It is true that I came here to choose a wife, but a princess? And how shall I choose?"

"Spend the day with them by the lake; then tell me tomorrow whom you have selected." They heard giggling, and suddenly three beautiful young women entered the throne room.

"Anna, the one in red, is my eldest," the king said. Then he indicated a girl dressed in a flowing green gown. "Beatrice is my second, and Cara my third." Cara was dressed all in blue.

"They are indeed lovely, sire," he said, unable to take his eyes off of the three fantastically beautiful women. "They look so alike."

"We are not alike in all ways," Anna said. "My hands can create great art, Beatrice can make any instrument sing, and Cara can outlast anyone at any sport. Come with us to the lake and you can get to know our talents."

Beside the lake, Anna spread several blankets on the grass and Lord Timothy made himself comfortable. The four shared a sumptuous meal, accompanied by rich ruby red wine. Relaxed, Timothy stretched out on the blanket.

"Let us show you our skills," Anna said. In turn, each woman kissed him full on the lips, tongues and lips caressing and entwining until he wasn't sure which one he was enjoying. Mouths covered his face and neck, nipping and sucking at his skin.

"You're wonderful," Beatrice said, "and any one of us would be happy to marry you. But in order for you to choose, we need to show you how we are different."

"My hands are where my talent lies," Anna said. She quickly removed Timothy's shirt and ran her palms down his hairy chest. She flicked a long fingernail over his flat nipple and heat slashed through him. She rubbed and scratched his shoulders and arms until he longed to reach out and hold her close. His skin was burning with need.

"My mouth is my talent," Beatrice said. While Anna stroked Timothy's upper body, Beatrice pulled off his boots and pants. She licked the tender skin of his inner thigh, then touched her tongue to the end of his erect cock. Slowly, she slid her lips down his erection until its entire length was in her warm, wet mouth.

"My body is my talent," Cara said. As she crouched over his face, Timothy realized that she had nothing on under her skirt. "I can hold myself poised over your mouth all day." She lowered her pussy until the smell of her filled his nostrils and his tongue reached for her clit. He licked the length of her slit, laving her wet flesh as he felt her move above him.

He couldn't believe the combination of sensations. Anna's hands caressed and scratched his chest, making his skin glow. "Yes," she said, "great art."

Beatrice's mouth played his cock like an instrument, creating harmonies he had never dreamt of. "The music of the ages," she whispered against his saliva-slick skin.

Cara's body was sensational, moving so his probing tongue could devour her. "I can make this last forever," she said, panting from the excitement.

Cara held back her climax until Timothy's cock erupted into Beatrice's mouth. Then she came, wetting his face with her juices.

"Oh, ladies," Timothy said later, when his breathing had calmed. "That was the most fantastic time I've ever had. But how can I possibly choose one of you to marry?"

"I would suggest," Anna said, "that you tell our father you need more time."

"What you don't know," Cara said, "is that we have a fourth sister, Dolly. She's married now, but before her husband chose, we kept the lord who is now her husband entertained for weeks. . . ."

# The Toll Bridge

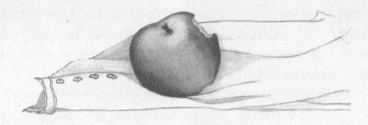

The two peasant girls sat at the top of the hill, gazing at the apple orchard on the other side of the fast-rushing stream. "Those apples are perfectly ripe," Maura said, tucking her bare feet beneath her full skirt.

"And so delicious," her friend Lydia said. "But to get there, we have to cross the footbridge." The two girls gazed at the rickety bridge and the gate at the far end. "And I'll bet Hugh will be at the other end, collecting his piece of silver for the toll." She thought of their empty pockets. "We could try to cross by using the rocks in the stream," she said.

"We could, but I've tried and fallen too many times." As they sat and stared at the apple trees heavy with ripe red fruit, Maura settled back on her elbows. "You know, Hugh's kind of cute. Maybe I could keep him occupied while you sneak across and collect enough apples for both of us." She handed Lydia her basket.

"Do you mean what I think you mean?"

Maura winked. "Why not? The few times I've seen him in town, he's looked at me as though he would be interested." She stood up, brushed bits of grass from her skirt, and trotted down the hill. "And he's adorable. I love men with dark skin and great muscles." With one hand on the rope handrail, she slowly made her way across the wooden slats, letting her hips sway as she walked.

"Hello, Maura," Hugh said as she reached him. "Are you here for apples? You have to pay the toll, you know."

"Maybe I'm not here for apples," she said, rubbing her hand up and down Hugh's muscular arm. "Maybe I'm here for you."

"Really?" he said, gazing down the front of Maura's oft-washed blouse into the shadowy valley between her lush, unrestrained breasts.

Maura trotted down the slope to the bank of the stream and placed her bare foot on a rock that was partly submerged. "Come walk with me."

Hugh made his way to the riverbank, pulled off his boots, and reached for Maura's hand. Together, they walked from rock to rock, toward the deep shadows under the bridge. "The water's very cold," Maura said as she waded through a shallow pool and sat in the shade on the bank.

Hugh sat beside her and rubbed his knuckle down her cheek. "And you're very warm." He kissed his fingertip, then rubbed it across her lips. "Very warm indeed."

Maura nipped the end of his finger, then wrapped her hand around the back of his neck and pulled him close. "Maybe we could stay warm together." She touched his lips with the tip of her tongue.

Quickly, he deepened the kiss, exploring the inside of her mouth with his tongue and tangling his fingers in her long brown hair. They moved their mouths, tasting and retasting until that wasn't enough. "Oh, Maura," Hugh groaned, sliding the blouse from her shoulders, baring her small, tight breasts tipped with large coffee-colored nipples, "I knew you'd be so beautiful."

Their hands and mouths were everywhere at

once. Hugh lifted and molded Maura's breasts, kissing the puckered tips while she unbuttoned his shirt and ran her hands over his skin, now slick with sweat. As he sucked at one nipple, she bit his muscular shoulder.

In no time, they were naked together, lying on a pallet Hugh had fashioned of an old blanket he'd found. In the bridge's shadow, their hands were always moving, stroking, squeezing, scratching. Maura found Hugh's hard shaft, wrapped her hand around it, and held tightly. At almost the same moment, Hugh found the soaking, hot lips of her cunt and slowly pressed two fingers inside.

"I can't wait any longer to feel you inside me," Maura cried, pulling him on top of her and pressing his erection against the opening of her cunt.

With one hard thrust, he was inside. "You're so hot and slippery, so ready for me!" he exclaimed as he pounded into her. She wrapped her legs around his waist and answered his every thrust with one of her own. "Oh yes," she cried.

"Oh yes," he screamed. Withdrawing to the edge of her body, he waited a moment, then pushed his length into her. He felt her muscles clench around his shaft as they both climaxed.

They rested until Hugh could speak again.

"That was wonderful," he said as they dressed. "Do you think your friend has enough apples by now?"

Maura gazed at him, then giggled. "You knew what I was doing?"

"Of course." Hugh laughed. "I don't make much money in tolls, but this job does have some very attractive fringe benefits."

# Magic in the Flames

Stare into the fire in your bedroom at exactly midnight on the eve of your eighteenth birthday and the flames will reveal the dream man who will make you happy forever. This legend had been told for generations.

Well, Marla thought, gazing into the flames, I'm here. Now what? She thought about Colin, the man she was to marry the next day, on her eighteenth birthday. What a dolt. A dullard. Boring in the extreme. "Show me my dream man," she said to the flames. With a great sigh, she settled comfortably onto the hearth rug and stared and stared. Soon, she was fast asleep before the fire.

She was dreaming. Fingers caressed her face, sliding over her closed eyes and lips. Gentle strokes covered her cheeks, her ears, and her jaw. Purring, she shifted so the hand could have better access to her skin. Although the hands were calloused and rough, the caresses were soft and very erotic.

In her dreams, the fingers stroked down her chest and began to unlace her nightgown. But was she truly dreaming? Marla opened her eyes, but the man was backlit by the dying flames. She could see only his shadowy outline.

"No," the man whispered. "Just feel." He brushed his fingertips over her eyes, closing the lids. He opened her robe, freeing her high, tight breasts. "Lovely," he whispered, his voice hoarse and low. He swirled his fingers over the velvety skin of her breasts, stroking toward their erect crests.

His mouth found one nipple and suckled, drawing the tight bud into his mouth as his tongue flicked the tip. "So delicious." He tongued the other breast, swirling his fingers over the one he had left slick with his saliva.

Marla needed more. The heat from the flames

was nothing compared with the heat flowing through her belly. "Please," she moaned.

"Oh yes, my love," the hoarse voice said. Quickly, he removed her gown. His rough palms covered her thighs and his fingers kneaded her flesh, opening her wet center. The hands moved closer and closer to the core of her hunger, brushing against the springy hair. "So wet, hungry for me." He sighed.

With one index finger, he roamed the folds of her pussy, delving deeply into every crevice, sliding through the slippery wetness. He parted her inner lips, stroking the gate of her being. "Open for me so I can know you completely."

"But I never . . ." Marla moaned.

"I know, but it's right for us now. And the flames know that I'm the man to make you happy forever."

She hesitated. "Yes," she said, parting her thighs. "Oh yes." His fingers invaded her body. She couldn't keep her hips from thrusting, trying to take the fingers more deeply into her.

She needed something, but she wasn't sure what. When the fingers left her, she felt lonely and empty. She opened her eyes and watched the shadow man remove his clothes. Then he positioned himself over her and drove his hardness into her.

She felt brief pain, then wonderful fullness and joy. "Yes," Marla cried as the man thrust into her over and over, easing her pain and replacing it with an incredible heat. She grasped his firm buttocks and pulled him more tightly against her. "Oh yes," she cried again as together they reached their climax and collapsed.

Later, the man stood and threw a large log onto the fire. As the flames blazed, she saw his face. "Colin," she cried. "You?"

"Yes, love. I've wanted you like this for so long, and I couldn't wait for tomorrow."

"The legend said that the flames would reveal my dream man. Is that you?"

"I hope so, for you have always been my dream woman." Later, he covered her with a quilt and left her dozing on the hearth rug. As the door closed, she smiled. The flames had been right. In only hours, she would marry her dream man.

I hope you enjoyed reading these bedtime stories as much as I enjoyed writing them.

As always, I welcome your reactions, so please write to me:

Joan Elizabeth Lloyd
c/o Warner Books
1271 Avenue of the Americas
New York, NY 10020